Toga in a Tangle

Written by Hawys Morgan

Illustrated by Mariano Epelbaum

Collins

1 Hide-and-seek

Felix stood behind the thick curtain. He shifted
uncomfortably in his heavy toga. He wished he could
at least hitch up the bottom of it to cool his legs down.
The summer evening air was warm and sticky, made
worse by the blazing torches dotted about all over
the villa.

He had been hiding here for what felt like ages. Hide-and-seek wasn't much fun if your friends didn't find you. His twin sister, Camilla, and their friend Livia were usually experts at finding his hiding places. However, they didn't normally play in a vast villa with a maze of corridors and rooms to hide in.

The sharp slap of leather sandals on tiles warned him someone was approaching. Maybe it was Camilla or Livia. He listened carefully and then stiffened when he realised these weren't light steps, they were heavy.

Two low voices whispered to one another. Whatever they were talking about, he wished they'd hurry up and move on. Felix wanted to get back to the banquet, the delicious food and his friends. He sank further into the safety of the curtain, wishing he'd chosen somewhere else to hide.

The voices grew closer and clearer.

"We have to do it tonight. It's our only chance," whispered one voice.

"But there are so many people at the banquet. We'll be seen," replied the other.

"The guests will be so busy eating and talking they won't notice us at all. It will be the perfect cover for our crime. You know where the jewellery is?" said the first voice.

Felix held his breath. Whoever these people were, they wouldn't be pleased to discover an eight-year-old boy listening to their secret conversation. Dust from the curtain was making his nose tickle. "Don't sneeze! Don't sneeze!" he told himself, scrunching up his nose.

The two voices moved away. Felix strained his ears, listening to the fading footsteps. When he was sure the coast was clear, he let himself breathe again. Then he sneezed – very loudly!

He didn't know exactly what those men were plotting, but he knew he needed to do something to stop it, and he knew he needed help.

2 Peace under threat

Felix wove his way through the crowds towards
the banqueting room. The air was heavy with the scent
of perfume. It felt like half of Rome was packed into
the villa. Laughter and noise spilt out of every door.
Felix scanned the flushed faces around him, looking for
his parents.

At last, he spotted his father's broad shoulders and dark curly hair. He was deep in conversation with his mother and a group of important-looking people. Felix and Camilla had been told clearly that they were not to bother their parents during the banquet, but this couldn't wait.

Felix sidled up to his father and pulled gently on his toga, but his father went on talking. He pulled a bit harder, but still his father didn't respond. Starting to feel a bit desperate, Felix yanked at the toga and pleaded, "Dad, please!"

His father spun around and looked down at him. "What is the meaning of this, Felix?" his father angrily muttered while trying to rearrange the folds of his toga. "How dare you interrupt me when I'm talking to some of my most important business partners?"

"We'll talk about your behaviour when we get home," said his mother, shaking her head. With that, his parents turned back to the grown-ups. Adults could be so frustrating. They never listened when you had something important to say.

The banqueting room heaved with people talking and laughing. Felix pushed his way through and came face to face with his sister, Camilla. Camilla popped the last of a boiled peacock egg in her mouth and swallowed. "The food here is amazing. Have you tried the oysters?" and she started to lead Felix towards a huge platter of oysters being carried into the room.

Felix shook off his sister and said, "There's no time to eat. We need to talk."

Camilla stopped dead in her tracks. "There's no time to eat?" she spluttered. "But you're always hungry! I've seen you eat a huge pile of pancakes and honey, cheese and olives and three boiled eggs for breakfast and then *still* stop off for some extra bread rolls on the way to school!"

At this point their friend Livia arrived. "There you are, Felix! We looked for you everywhere. In the end, we gave up," she said. "Why the grumpy face? Have they run out of oysters?"

"Come on, you lot. I need your help. It's urgent." Felix led the others outside to the deserted atrium and rapidly told them what he'd overheard.

12

When he'd finished, Livia shook her head, worried. "My mother told me about some jewellery here at the villa. She said there's a golden necklace and a pair of earrings studded with precious jewels. They're a gift for Mosi, the Egyptian ambassador."

Livia paced the courtyard. "Egypt and Rome have been at war for many years. The jewellery is supposed to be a sign of friendship and peace between the two empires. If it goes missing, the Egyptians will think we are rude. We have to stop these men from taking it."

The children looked into the calm waters of the pool, thinking about their next steps.

"We should tell Maximus, the senator," said Camilla.

"If even Mum and Dad wouldn't listen to me, what makes you think the senator will?" replied Felix.

"You're right, Felix," said Livia. "None of the grown-ups will believe us. They'll just think we're playing a silly game and making it up. We have to stop them ourselves."

But how could they stop them when they didn't know the plotters' names, or even what they looked like?

"We don't know who the plotters are, but we *do* know what they want," said Livia.

"The jewellery! That's it!" exclaimed Camilla. "We need to find out where the jewels are kept and wait there until the thieves arrive. But what then?"

"I know! We could use a big catapult to fire ostrich eggs at them!" exclaimed Felix.

"Nice idea, but we haven't got a catapult," said Livia.

"What if we protect the jewels with a pit of poisonous snakes?" suggested Camilla.

"Even if we find some snakes, there's no way I'm going to touch one," said Felix, shuddering at the thought.

14

"I've got it! How about we balance a bucket of frogs on the door? When the thieves open the door, the bucket will fall on them and they'll be covered in slimy frogs!" suggested Livia.

For a moment, the children thought they had a plan, but then Camilla pointed out that real villains wouldn't be put off by a few frogs.

Livia sighed. "This is hopeless. How on earth will we stop them?"

"We'll think of something," said Felix. "We always do. First things first – let's find out where the jewels are. We can't do anything until we know that."

And with that, they headed back into the heat of the banquet to hunt for information.

15

3 The silver casket

Felix spied his grandmother's friend, Antonia, across the room. Antonia waved and started to make her way towards them. Felix's shoulders drooped. Antonia loved to test Camilla and Felix on their times tables, but maybe she had the information they needed.

"Camilla and Felix! How smart you look for once. And good evening, Livia. It's always a pleasure to see you." The old woman bowed her head to them.

"Antonia," said Camilla, "how lovely to see you! We've got a question for you."

"Ah! But first I have a question for you – five times eight?"

"40," Felix groaned. "Now our question. Livia's been telling us about some precious jewellery in this villa. Do you know where it is? We're terribly interested in jewellery."

"Really?" replied Antonia, surprised. "Well, this jewellery is among the finest ever made. Pure, brilliant gold from Hispania, surrounding teardrop pearls and dazzling green emeralds from the East. But you can't see them. They're locked away safely in a casket. Our senator, Maximus, will present them to the Egyptian ambassador at the end of the banquet. The ambassador will take them back to Egypt as a gift for the pharaoh.

I wouldn't be surprised if such magnificent jewels ended up in a pyramid with a mummy."

Camilla frowned, confused. "What's a mummy?" she asked.

Antonia smiled and replied patiently: "When an important Egyptian dies, they wrap the body up in strips of linen and this is called a mummy. Then they bury the mummy in a big pyramid surrounded by valuable things."

"Ooh, I hope I'm important enough to be buried with jewels!" dreamt Livia.

"Goodness," said Camilla. "Making mummies sounds like a lot of work."

Felix sighed a little impatiently, eager to get back to the question of the jewels. "Antonia, do you know where the casket is?" he asked.

"Hmm, why should you want to know?" replied Antonia, suspiciously. "Well, I don't know for sure, but I expect it would be kept in Maximus's office."

Luckily, at that moment, a troupe of dancers and musicians started to perform in the middle of the room. The loud strings and pipes stopped Antonia asking any awkward questions. They waved goodbye to her and fought their way through the crowds to the hallway. There was no time to lose. The jewellery might have been stolen already.

19

They ran through the cool empty hallways of the villa. It felt quiet after the noise of the banquet. Livia knew exactly where the office was. She'd seen its closed tall wooden doors when she'd been searching for Felix in their earlier game of hide-and-seek.

They ran around a corner and there it was, but now the doors were ajar. Light from a flaming torch danced across the entrance, casting long shadows up the walls.

They crept up to the doorway and peered in. Two large figures were hunched over a small casket. It was impossible to see their faces. They were trying to force the casket open using a knife. How on earth could they stop these grown men? Grown men who had a knife!

Camilla and Felix's eyes met, and they whispered one word to each other: toga.

4 Toga in a tangle

That morning, Felix had gone to the baths with his
father as usual. After a quick clean, he'd played board
games and chatted with his father. It was then that
his father had told Felix that he and Camilla were old
enough to accompany their parents to an important
banquet, and that meant Felix had to wear a toga for
the first time.

Once home, his father had presented Felix with a neatly folded toga. It was so heavy, Felix staggered backwards when it was placed in his arms. His father showed him how to stretch out the fabric and drape one end over a shoulder, before passing the rest of the fabric around his back, under his right arm, and then over the left shoulder and arm again. Felix could barely move under the heavy, uncomfortable fabric.

Felix was left to practise putting on the toga by himself. He kept getting confused between his left and his right. He couldn't remember whether it went over the shoulder or round his back first. It had looked so easy when Dad had done it.

Hearing his cries of frustration, Camilla came to see what the fuss was about. She tried to help, but only made things worse. They ended up in  a great big tangle on the floor. The fabric seemed to go on for ever. They had laid there giggling, until Mum had come and told them off for getting creases in the toga.

Well, maybe the silly toga would save the day.

With Livia and Camilla's help, Felix unwound his toga. It was a relief for Felix to stand in his cool linen tunic after all those hours of being weighed down.

Dad thought he was grown-up enough to wear a toga. Now was the time to show him that being grown-up wasn't about what you wore, it was about how you acted.

Felix indicated to Camilla to creep to the other side of
the doorway. He peered around the edge of the door
to make sure the men weren't looking their way, and
then he threw one end of the toga to Camilla.
They pulled the toga flat across the doorway and
crouched, listening hard. Livia pressed herself to the edge
of the doorway and watched, ready to give the signal.

The men laughed with satisfaction as they finally managed to force the casket open. Livia spied the men hiding the jewellery inside the thick folds of their togas before both men turned and made their way to the door.

Livia nodded at the others, and silently mouthed: "*One, two, three!*" As one, they jumped to their feet pulling the toga tight across the doorway just as the men were passing through.

Crash! Two heavy bodies crashed to the ground like felled trees, roaring in angry surprise.

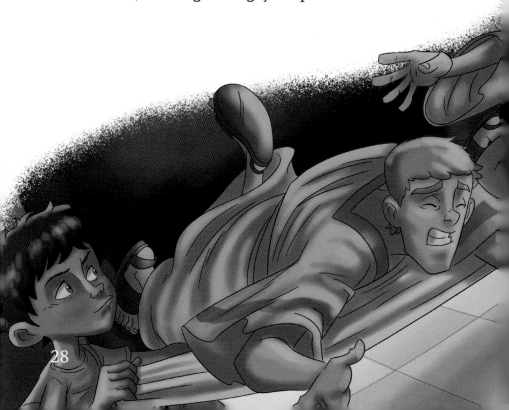

Quick as a flash, the children wrapped the toga around the men until they were covered from head to toe and unable to move even a little finger.

5 The truth comes out

The shouting and crashing had caught the attention of the banquet guests who crowded around them chattering in shocked surprise.

Camilla and Felix's father pushed his way to the front and stood, looking aghast at the chaos the children had caused. "What have you done?" he cried.

Maximus, the senator, and Mosi, the Egyptian
ambassador, arrived at the scene. Felix bravely took a
step forward and bowed deeply. "My lords, if you look
in the office, you will see that the jewellery has gone."

Maximus looked beyond the children into the room
and saw the broken casket. He turned back to
the children. "Go on."

Livia gestured to the bandaged figures on the floor. "Bound in here, you'll find the jewellery and the thieves."

Mosi stepped forward and looked at the bundle with a small smile. "Just like the mummies we have at home. You've done a fine job of binding these bodies."

Maximus called his head guard and angrily shouted:
"How has a thief entered my villa? I thought I'd made
it clear that we needed tight security this evening.
If it were not for these brave children, common
thieves would have stolen these priceless gifts.
Unwind them now!"

Maximus watched gravely as the bundle was unwound.

There was a sharp intake of breath from the onlookers as the two men struggled to their feet, rubbing their eyes.

"There ... there must be some mistake!" Maximus stammered. "You're clearly playing a trick. These are my brothers, Tertius and Quintus."

The men dusted off their togas and smiled uncertainly at the senator. "Maximus, our dear eldest brother. What an outrage to be treated this way at your house by these dreadful children. We demand you punish them!"

Anger pulsed through Felix's body. "It was definitely you! I heard you plotting. I recognise your voice. We saw you!"

Felix and Camilla's father stepped forward and put a protective hand on their shoulders. "Sir, my children are no liars."

"May I suggest," said Mosi calmly, "that Tertius and Quintus allow themselves to be searched? To avoid any doubt, you understand. You would not object, would you, gentlemen?"

The two men shuffled their feet and looked nervously from one to the other.

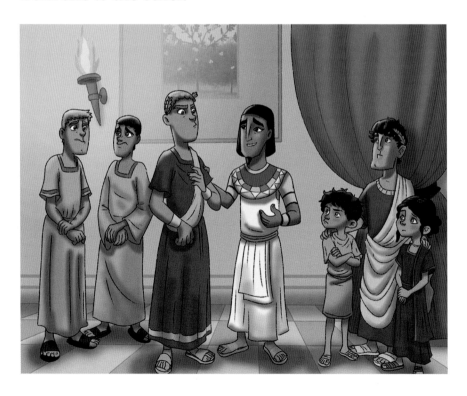

Without a word, Maximus reached out and patted down the folds of their togas. He fished out the necklace and the earrings, the beautiful jewels glinting in the torchlight. He turned away in disgust. "Take them away, guards!"

Tertius and Quintus were led away, shouting angrily.

Camilla and Felix's mother led Maximus to a quiet
bench outside in the garden. The children followed.

Maximus shook his head and sadly explained: "I was
the eldest, the best student and my parents' favourite.
My brothers were always playing mean tricks on me:
hiding my school scrolls so I'd get in trouble, putting
salt on my honey cakes ... you know the kind of thing.
When I became a senator, I made sure Tertius and
Quintus always had everything they needed, but they
hated my success. I knew they were jealous, but I never
thought they'd go so far as to risk the peace of Rome
and Egypt, just to get back at me."

Mosi took Maximus by the shoulders and said, "Gifts won't secure peace between Egypt and Rome, but friendship will." The two men smiled at each other warmly.

Then Mosi turned to the group of children.
"Thank you for your quick thinking and bravery.
I was most impressed. Here, I have some gifts for you
all the way from Egypt." He handed them a beautifully
carved toy hippo, a clockwork dog and a model horse.
"You must visit me in Egypt. You clearly have great skills
when it comes to making mummies!"

Their laughter was interrupted by a great rumble. Felix blushed. "Ahem, excuse me. With all this detective work, I haven't had any dinner."

Felix, Camilla and Livia headed back to the banquet. Thankfully, the banqueting table was still piled high with delicious food.

"Snails – my favourite!" exclaimed Livia, helping herself.

Felix couldn't decide where to start.
With the roast swan? Or the stuffed dormice?
Then he saw them – honey cakes! After the
evening he'd had, nobody could blame him
for starting with dessert first!

A letter to Egypt

Glorious Pharaoh, leader of the mighty
Egyptian empire!

I send you good news from Rome. Peace between our
two empires is confirmed!

Senator Maximus planned a delicious banquet.
Plotters tried to derail our peace plans, but three plucky
Roman children stopped them. We could all learn much
from their bravery and determination.

On my return, I will bring a generous gift from
Senator Maximus, and a recipe for some very tasty
honey cakes!

Your humble servant,

Mosi

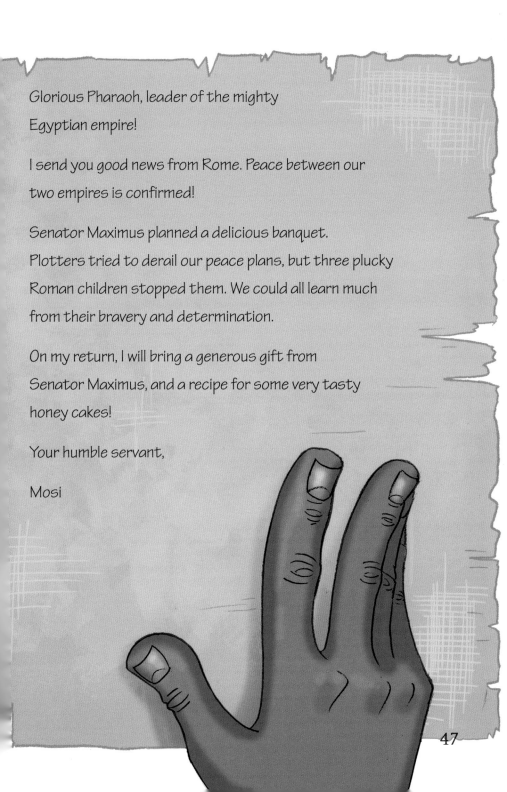

Ideas for reading

Written by Clare Dowdall, PhD
Lecturer and Primary Literacy Consultant

Reading objectives:
- discuss the sequence of events in books and how items of information are related
- discuss and clarify the meanings of words, linking new meanings to known vocabulary
- make inferences on the basis of what is being said and done

Spoken language objectives:
- ask relevant questions to extend their understanding and knowledge
- use relevant strategies to build their vocabulary

- give well-structured descriptions and explanations

Curriculum links: History

Word count: 3000

Interest words: toga, banquet, plotters, villa, atrium, ambassador, empire, senator, catapult, casket, pharaoh, pyramid, mummy, troupe, derail, plucky, determination, humble

Resources: whiteboard, sticky notes, card and pens/pencils for making menu cards, ICT to research honey cake recipes and Roman clothing

Build a context for reading

- Read the title of the story. Ask children if they know what a toga is, and who wore them.
- Explain that the story is set in ancient Rome, in Italy, a long time ago. Ask children if they know anything about the Romans and their civilisation e.g. knowledge about Roman inventions.
- Read the blurb to the children and ask them to explain what a banquet and a plot are.
- Introduce and discuss the vocabulary from the list above to provide context for reading.

Understand and apply reading strategies

- Read Chapter 1 together. Ask children to try to build a picture in their head of the setting and events that unfold.
- Challenge children to recount the opening of the story to a partner, then ask the pairs to raise three questions that they hope to answer